There's No Such Thing as a Chanukah Bush, Sandy Goldstein

Susan Sussman *pictures by* Charles Robinson

ALBERT WHITMAN & COMPANY, NILES, ILLINOIS

Special thanks to my editor, Kathleen Tucker

Library of Congress Cataloging in Publication Data

Sussman, Susan.
    There's no such thing as a Chanukah bush, Sandy
Goldstein.

    Summary: A wise, understanding grandfather helps
Robin, a Jewish child, cope with Christmas; not an easy
task when even Sandy, who is also Jewish, is allowed
to have a Christmas tree and Robin can't have one.
    [1. Christmas—Fiction.   2. Jews—Fiction]
I. Robinson, Charles, 1931- ill. II. Title.
PZ7.S9657Th 1983   [Fic]   83-1291
ISBN 0-8075-7862-2 (lib. bdg.)

Text © 1983 by Susan Sussman
Illustrations © 1983 by Charles Robinson
Published in 1983 by Albert Whitman & Company, Niles, Illinois
Published simultaneously in Canada by
General Publishing, Limited, Toronto

12   11   10   9   8   7   6   5

For my mother and father
and in loving memory of my grandfather,
Sidney Rissman

Contents

1
Oh, No! Not *That* Question!

I hid inside the front door of my apartment building. Through the window I could see Heather. She was pacing back and forth in front of her building.

I usually pick her up at 8:30. This morning I was going to be late. On purpose.

When my watch read 8:45, I threw open the door and ran toward her.

"Come on!" I said. "We're late!" I grabbed her arm and pulled her along with me. "Why do I always have to wait for you?"

"Ha-ha, Robin, that's very funny," said

Heather. She ran with me. "You don't have . . . Sister Anne yelling at you . . . if you come to school just one . . . second late."

"I'll trade . . . my Miss Sullivan for . . . your Sister Anne . . . any day," I gasped, trying to catch my breath.

We raced in silence across Duffy's

Used Car Lot and down three alleys. It was too hard for us to talk and run at the same time. Which is *exactly* what I wanted. I didn't want to give Heather time to ask me *that* question.

I prayed the traffic light at Devon Avenue would be green. I would run across the street to P.S. 43 while Heather turned west to St. Francis. We rounded the corner—just as the light turned red.

"Do . . . you . . . have . . . your . . . tree yet?" asked Heather as soon as she had stopped.

There it was! *That* question. Same time every year. Only this year it was worse because of what Sandy Goldstein had done.

I gasped, coughed, and gasped again. I was pretending I couldn't catch my breath. I was stalling for time.

"Well, Robin?" said Heather.

"Heather . . . you . . . know . . . that I . . . can't have . . . a Christmas tree."

"Well, Sandy Goldstein has a Chanukah bush. She told me you're allowed to have a Chanukah bush."

"There's no such thing as a Chanukah bush," I said.

The traffic light turned green. I dashed across the street.

"What about Sandy Goldstein?" yelled Heather.

"Jews don't have Christmas trees," I yelled back.

"Sandy Goldstein's Jewish," Heather screamed over the four lanes of rush-hour traffic. "Isn't she?"

I cupped my hand to my ear and shook my head. It was our signal that we could no longer hear over the noise of the cars.

But I *had* heard. Sandy Goldstein *is* Jewish. And I hated her for having a Chanukah bush when *I* really wanted one.

2

It's Just the *Worst* School Day of the Whole Entire Year

School was awful!

Miss Sullivan let the entire fourth-grade class make Christmas ornaments. All morning!

I took a white styrofoam ball, a box of pins, and a bunch of sequins. I went to the back of the room and plopped down on the floor. I put a pin through a green sequin and stuck it into the ball. Hard. "Take *that*, Sandy Goldstein," I whispered. I took another pin and a red sequin and stabbed the ball again.

Our usually neat classroom was a jumble of paste, glitter, ribbons, colored paper, sequins, styrofoam balls, and tinsel. Miss Sullivan, who usually hates noisy classrooms, sat talking and making ornaments with the rest of us. Right next to her— practically sitting in her lap!—was Sandy Goldstein. She was cutting and gluing colored strips of paper, making the world's ugliest paper chain.

I worked silently. Listening. Everyone was talking at once.

"Santa's going to bring me . . . "

"If Santa forgets the batteries for my toys again this year, I'm gonna stop leaving him cookies."

"We have the most beautiful angel on top of our tree. Her halo touches the ceiling."

"My mom says that if my dad picks out a skinny tree one more time . . . "

"We have so many presents under our

tree that I bet we don't finish opening them 'til New Year's."

By the end of the morning I had stuck 325 sequins into my Sandy Goldstein styrofoam ball.

That afternoon we practiced Christmas carols. I just mouthed the words. I didn't know if Jews were supposed to sing the words "little Lord Jesus" and " 'ron yon Virgin." I did sing "Jingle Bells" and "White Christmas." They seemed safe.

Miss Sullivan showed us the movie *Christmas Around the World*. We saw children in Japan, Australia, France, Africa, and Denmark celebrating Christmas. I wondered why no one had made a film called *Chanukah Around the World*. I didn't watch the movie. I drew pictures of Christmas trees on my desk, instead.

We ended the day by stringing cranberries and popcorn to decorate the classroom windows. I stuck my finger three times trying to push the needle through the cranberries. My popcorn kept breaking off the string.

Miss Sullivan told us we could take our ornaments home. I stuck my Sandy Goldstein styrofoam ball in my coat pocket. Maybe if my parents saw how beautiful the sequins looked they would think about having a Chanukah bush. Maybe . . .

By the time the 3:00 bell rang, I made up my mind that I had to at least *ask* for a Chanukah bush.

I raced home and ran up the apartment stairs two at a time. I stopped outside my door. My heart was pounding so hard! I took a deep breath, put on a huge smile, and burst inside.

3
A Cookie with a Bite Out of It Is *Not* a Christmas Tree

"Mom! Mom!" I called.

"In here, honey."

I ran to the dining room. My mother was sitting at the table, cleaning the menorah. "Hi, sweetheart," she said. "This is almost ready for you."

I slid into the chair across from her. She was using toothpicks to scrape off bits of candle wax left from the last night's Chanukah celebration. I knew in my heart this wasn't a good time to ask my question. But I couldn't stop myself.

"Mom," I said. I tried to make my voice sound as excited and happy as possible. "Sandy Goldstein has a Chanukah bush!"

14

"That's nice, dear," she said.

What kind of answer was that?! Mom could have said, "God will strike her dead," or "Sandy is a bad person," or even "What a lovely idea. Perhaps we should get one." What could I say to, "That's nice, dear"?

My mother looked up at me with her soft eyes and gentle smile. "Go hang up your coat and have your snack. Then the menorah will be ready for you to arrange the candles."

I hung my coat on the kitchen hook. The sequined ornament fell out of my pocket onto the floor. Quickly, I picked it up and put it back. I didn't think I should show it to my mother. Not just then. I took an apple from the refrigerator and brought it to the table with me.

Mom handed me the box of Chanukah candles, and I spilled them out onto the table. My grandparents still used the old-fashioned orange Chanukah candles. My mother and I liked the newer colored ones. There were white, pink, yellow, blue, green, and red candles. Each night I tried different color combinations.

Mom went to the sofa and began knitting. The apartment was very quiet. I moved the candles around on the table, trying to find six colors I liked. Red, white, blue, red, white, blue. White, white, white, red, red, red. They all looked terrible!

"Can we have a Chanukah bush?" I asked softly. I felt warm tears float up into my eyes.

"There is no such thing," she said. Her knitting needles clicked quickly. I pushed the candles around some more. I decided to try again.

"But Sandy Goldstein has . . . "

"What Sandy Goldstein has is a Christmas tree. And you know Jews do not believe in Christmas."

My tears were the large kind that creep slowly down the cheek. They rested on the corners of my mouth.

"Sandy's Jewish," I said. My nose was all stuffy. Mom didn't seem to notice.

Her knitting needles were really clicking fast. Then, suddenly, they stopped. Mom sighed a very deep sigh.

"You're right, Robin," she said. "Sandy *is* Jewish. But there are many ways of being Jewish. In our own family there are men who wear hats, always, to show their respect for God."

"Like Uncle Bob?"

"Yes. And there are men who worship in synagogues where the men pray bareheaded."

"Uncle Marshall?"

"Yes. And your father prefers to cover his head during prayer. All three have found their own way to be Jewish.

"If Sandy Goldstein's parents feel they can live with a Christmas tree, then that is their business. But I will not have one in my home."

I stuck white candles into the menorah. I hated the white candles.

At sundown, I lit a candle and used it to light the other five in the menorah. We all sang the blessing and sat down to dinner.

I did not mention the Chanukah bush to my father. He was much more religious than my mother. Every morning, while I ate breakfast, I could hear him praying in his bedroom. If my mother wouldn't let me have a Chanukah bush, there was no way my father would.

After dinner, mom held up the Chanukah gift bag, and I reached in for that night's present. It was a key chain shaped like a cookie with a bite out of it. A shiny brass key to our apartment was on it.

"Thank you," I said, trying to look happy. I had wanted my own key, and I really did love the key chain. But they didn't stop me from wanting a Chanukah bush.

At bedtime, Mom came into my room. She tucked the covers around me. She stroked a cool hand over my forehead. "Grandpa just called," she said. "He's coming for dinner tomorrow night."

I didn't say anything. I could be a real pain when I wanted to.

"He says he has a surprise for you," she said. I still didn't say anything. Mom sighed. She bent down and kissed my cheek. "Sleep well, Sunshine." She left the door open a crack, the way I like it.

Hot tears came again and I sobbed into my pillow. I cried so hard my back hurt. My pillow got all wet. My nose was so stuffy I couldn't breathe. I blew it over and over until it was rubbed raw. I used up a whole half box of tissues.

It isn't easy being Jewish at Christmas time.

4
The Surprise of the Ear-Wiggler

My parents were in the kitchen. Mom was preparing the coffee and dessert, and Dad was washing the dinner dishes.

Grandpa and I sat alone at the dining-room table. He was trying to teach me how to make my ears wiggle and my hair move back and forth. The month before he had taught me how to lift just one eyebrow at a time. This new ear-hair trick seemed like it was going to be a lot harder to learn.

"How would you like to go to a Christmas party with me tomorrow?" Grandpa asked. "Just you and me?" He wiggled his ears at me.

I looked up at him. Was he testing me?

"Well?" he said. He is a big man with a strong booming voice. I was afraid my parents would hear. Had my mother told him about my wanting a Chanukah bush?

"I . . . Jews don't believe in Christmas," I said. I searched his face to see if I'd given the right answer.

"Well, well, well," he laughed. He lifted one thick eyebrow at me. "Christmas may not be a *Jewish* holiday. But when I see all the trees and lights and hear all the carols, why then I must believe it is *somebody's* holiday."

My father brought the dessert dishes to the table and sat down with us. Grandpa took out a cigar.

"And I also believe," said Grandpa, "that my union is having a Christmas party tomorrow for all the members and their families." He slipped the paper ring off his cigar and slid it onto my thumb.

Grandpa's doctor wouldn't let him smoke anymore but he still liked holding a cigar after dinner.

"Grandpa helped plan the party," said Mom. She poured a glass of milk for me and coffee for the adults.

I didn't understand. Why had Grandpa planned a Christmas party for his union? If Jews didn't celebrate Christmas, why was Grandpa helping others celebrate? But I didn't dare ask. I didn't want him to change his mind about inviting me to the party.

Grandpa stirred a teaspoon of his coffee into my glass of milk. I was allowed to have coffee-milk when Grandpa came.

"So? Do we have a date tomorrow?" Grandpa asked.

I glanced at my parents. They were smiling.

"I guess so." I shrugged.

The sky did not fall on me.

5

The Tap-dancingest, Tree-trimmingest, Chimney-eatingest Christmas Party Ever!

A huge sign in the hotel lobby said:

GARMENT WORKERS
Local 61
CHRISTMAS PARTY
1:00-5:00
GRAND BALLROOM

Grandpa wrapped his large hand around mine and led me to the elevators. I was wearing the black velvet party dress my cousin Martha had given me. I usually hate the clothes she hands down. The colors are dull and the styles are dumb. But this dress was beautiful. It had a full skirt that spun way out when I twirled.

24

It was cold outside but there was no snow. Mom said that if I wore tights I didn't have to wear boots. I had on my black patent party shoes. When I walked on the sidewalk or a wood floor I could make my shoes sound like a tap dancer's. I hoped the Grand Ballroom wasn't carpeted.

"You look bee-yoo-tee-ful!" said Grandpa. He always says I look bee-yoo-tee-ful. He said it even when I had the chicken pox. This time, though, I thought he might be right.

A loud band was blasting "Rudolph the Red-nosed Reindeer" as we stepped off the elevator. I gripped Grandpa's hand. We tried to make our way through the crowd of people outside the ballroom. We had to move slowly. Everyone seemed to want to stop and shake Grandpa's hand. He knew all of their names. He introduced everyone to me. I looked at the floor and didn't say anything. I'm shy around people I don't know. I wondered if they could tell this was my first Christmas party. I gripped Grandpa's hand tighter.

Finally, we entered the Grand Ballroom. Grandpa picked me up so I could see. It was like a huge circus! There were bright lights and decorations everywhere. Bubbles from a bubble-making machine flew up and around the room. Red and green balloons were all over the ceiling, and kids were popping the ones that floated down.

There were two stages. Ten musicians dressed as elves sat on one stage and played Christmas songs. On the other stage were five of the biggest, most beautiful Christmas trees I'd ever seen. Boxes of tinsel and ornaments sat under them. People walking by grabbed handfuls of tinsel and threw them onto the trees. Some people jumped right up on stage and hung up an ornament or two.

Food tables lined one side of the room.

They were covered with cookies and cakes and candy canes and gingerbread houses and bowls of punch.

Huge boxes of popcorn were on the floor. A woman dressed like Mrs. Claus was helping a bunch of little kids glue paper chain decorations.

"What's your pleasure, Princess?" asked Grandpa.

I looked around the crowded room. I wanted to do *everything*. But I felt too shy to do *anything*.

"Oh," I said, "I'll just watch."

Suddenly Grandpa whisked me up into the air and swung me over to the dance floor. He set me down so my feet were on his shoes. We danced to "We Wish You a Merry Christmas."

The dance floor was made of nice hard wood. When the band started playing "You better watch out, you better not cry . . . ," I started to click my heels and swirl around.

My shoes made a super tapping sound and my dress spun way out. Grandpa clicked and swirled right along with me.

"You are a bee-yoo-tee-ful dancer," he said.

"So are you," I said. We danced through "Deck the halls with boughs of holly . . . " and "Jingle bells, jingle bells . . . . " I could have kept dancing, but Grandpa thought we should have some punch.

I was so hot from dancing that I had three cups of punch. Grandpa helped me break off part of a gingerbread-house chimney. Then he lifted me up onto the Christmas tree stage and watched me put tinsel on one of the trees. I tried to cover up the empty spots. I did a pretty good job for my first time.

Grandpa had some people to say hello to. He said I could keep decorating or dancing or eating. He showed me where he would be when I was ready to go home.

I was so busy putting tinsel on the tree that I didn't understand why people began yelling and screaming. I looked up. There, coming through the crowd, was Santa Claus!

He had a gigantic sack on his back. A big chair had been set up for him on the stage where the musicians were. It took all ten of them to push and pull Santa up onto the stage. Santa put the sack down next to his chair and sat down. As he untied the sack, I could see hundreds of small pink and blue bags inside.

All around me kids raced to get into line. I looked for Grandpa. He was standing across the room. I waved until he saw me. He smiled and waved back. I pointed to Santa Claus. Grandpa nodded and smiled. In a flash, I jumped off the Christmas tree stage and got in line.

6

A Funny Friend and a Minty Santa

"What are you going to ask for?" said the girl in front of me. She had two long blond pigtails. One was braided with green ribbon, the other with red.

"I . . . I don't know," I said. I hadn't thought about asking for anything. I just knew Santa Claus would hand me a bag like those he was giving the other kids in line. I had never sat on Santa's lap before. I wondered if it was all right for me to ask for something.

"Well, I'm asking for a wood-burning set," she said. "Did you ever use one?"

"Yes, I . . . "

"Aren't they great! My friend uses his to mark his name and phone number on everything. I mean, his mitt, bat, shoes, bedroom door. E-V-E-R-Y-T-H-I-N-G. And don't you just love that *smell* of burning wood?"

She talked as fast as the words could come out. I liked listening to her. She didn't seem to mind that I felt shy. I don't think she even noticed. In no time at all we were next in line for Santa.

My new friend hopped right up on Santa's lap.

"Hi ya, Santa," she said.

"Ho, ho, ho," he said. "And what is your name?"

"Julieanne. You can call me Julie."

"And what can Santa bring you, Julie?"

"A wood-burning set," she said. "The Willie Woodsman Deluxe Model, if you can. It has that safety holder so I won't burn my fingers."

"Ah-ha," he said. "Anything else?"

"Well, that's what I want most. But I'd sure appreciate it if you could make Freddie Murray notice me. He's in the fifth grade and he is C-U-T-E, cute."

"Well, Julie, I'll certainly do my best. Meanwhile, here's a little present from me to you." He reached into his sack and pulled out a pink paper bag.

"Thanks, Santa," Julie said. She hopped off his lap. "I'll wait for you over here," she said to me.

Then it was my turn. My heart was pounding so hard I could feel it in my ears. Would Santa mind that I was Jewish? Could he tell?

"Don't be shy, child," he smiled. He patted his knee. He had kind eyes and I liked his smile.

I climbed up onto his knee. He smelled like my father does after he shaves. It's a nice minty smell.

"That's a good girl. Now, what's your name?"

"Robin," I said. I could see where Santa's beard was hooked on behind his ears. I pretended not to notice. I didn't think that would be polite.

"And what can Santa bring you for Christmas?"

I took a deep breath. "Peace on earth, good will to men," I said. I figured that was safe. Not like asking for a Christmas present or anything.

Santa tilted his head to one side. "Well, well, well. I do believe I am working on that as my gift to the *world*. But what I want to know is what I can bring *you*."

"Well," I said, taking a very deep breath, "if it's not too much trouble, I'd like a pair of white figure skates, size four, with bells on the laces and blade guards." I was hoping to get skates for my birthday. But that was a whole month and a half away.

"That's a fine thing to ask for." Santa smiled. "I'll see what I can do. Meanwhile"— he reached into the sack and pulled out a pink bag—"here is a little something for right now."

"Thank you, Santa Claus," I said. The words felt strange in my mouth.

7

Diamond Rings and Bunny Hops and Prayers That Don't Come True

"Let's see what you got," said Julie. We sat down on the edge of the stage and looked into my bag. There was a pin with two small pine cones and a sprig of holly. Julie was already wearing hers. I pinned mine on. It was beautiful on the black velvet dress.

I reached into the bag again. There was a ring with a blue diamond in it. It was too big for my fingers.

"Here," said Julie. "Just squeeze the back and it gets smaller." She held up her hand to show me her ring. "Mine has a yellow diamond in it."

There was also a small magnifying glass and a pencil covered in purple velvet.

"Wanna trade?" Julie asked. "I *love* purple! I got a blue pencil."

I love blue so we traded.

The band began playing the Bunny Hop. I had learned the steps in gym class. "Oh, let's dance," I said.

"I don't know how to do that one," said Julie.

"It's easy. I'll teach you." We hid our bags behind a curtain and ran to the dance floor. We danced the Bunny Hop, and then the band played the Mexican Hat Dance. Julie taught it to me. I made my shoes click like a Spanish dancer's. Julie held her arms up over her head and snapped her fingers while she danced.

The band finished playing and a man climbed on stage. "Ladies and gentlemen, boys and girls, and Santa Claus. Thank you all for coming and making this a very special Christmas. We will now have the drawing for the five trees."

"Oh I hope I win I hope I win I hope I win," said Julie. She clasped her hands in front of her and squeezed her eyes shut tight. It looked like she was praying.

"How can people win a tree?" I asked.

She opened one eye in my direction. "Didn't you fill out an entry blank at the door?" she asked.

I shook my head sadly.

"It's too late now!" she said. "D-R-A-T, drat!"

"Oh, that's O.K. I can't have a tree, anyway. I'm Jewish." I tried to sound as if I didn't really care.

"Oh, good." She smiled. "Then you can help *me* pray for one."

I didn't see any harm in that. We both gripped our hands together and prayed. But none of the five names the man picked out of the bowl was Julie's.

"Well, we tried," she said. We went to get our bags from behind the curtain.

"How come you don't have a tree?" I asked. I thought everyone who wasn't Jewish had a tree.

"Too expensive," she said. "This year, anyway. Maybe next year . . . " She looked sad. I didn't mean to make her unhappy.

I guess *I* started looking sad because Julie suddenly laughed and said, "You should see what my mom did! She took all the plants in the house and put them on the table near the front window. Then she strung them with lights and we all put on ornaments we made. It looks G-R-E-A-T, great!"

We saw a line of children near the Christmas tree stage. We joined them, and a woman gave each of us some tinsel and two ornaments to take home. I gave mine to Julie.

Her dad came to get her. We said good-bye. I found Grandpa and told him I was ready to go home.

8
A Two-and-a-half-cent Thought

"Well?" asked Grandpa as we drove home. "What did you think?"

"I think I absolutely, positively, looove Christmas parties," I said.

"What's not to like?" he said, raising his left eyebrow.

We drove in silence for a while.

"Two and a half cents for your thoughts," said Grandpa.

"Grandpa, it's 'a penny for your thoughts'!"

Grandpa winked at me. "Mine are worth a penny. Yours are worth at least two and a half cents."

I laughed. "Grandpa, why is it all right for me to go with you to a Christmas party but not all right for me to" —I decided to just say it—"to have a Christmas tree at home?"

We drove a while before he answered.

"I think," he said, "there is a difference between celebrating something because *you* believe in it, and helping friends celebrate something because *they* believe in it.

"Your friend Heather Patterson and her parents came to your house on Passover. They ate the matzos. They helped read the story of Passover. They shared our delicious Seder food. You honored them by inviting them to share in something very beautiful to you. Right?"

"Right," I said.

"But did that make them Jewish? Did they run home and throw out all the bread and cake from their home like we do on Passover? Did they change their regular dishes for Passover dishes?"

"Grandpa!" I laughed.

"Just so. And if you share in a friend's Christmas does that make you a Christian? Do you run home and throw away your menorah and Chanukah candles and put up a Christmas tree?"

We pulled up in front of my building. The lights on the tree in the courtyard twinkled. Most of the apartments had trees in the front windows. Hundreds of tiny lights winked and blinked and glittered.

"Christmas trees are so pretty," I said.

"Yes, they are. Which is why we are lucky when we have friends who will share theirs with us."

"I love you, Grandpa," I said. I gave him a big kiss and a hug.

"I love you, too, Bee-yoo-tee-ful." He waited until I was safely inside the door, then blew me a kiss. I caught it and blew one back to him. He caught it and put it in his pocket to take home.

9
The Sharing

The next day I asked Heather if she could come over to my house for dinner. It was the last night of Chanukah and I wanted her to celebrate it with me.

She helped me arrange the candles in the menorah. There were nine candles left in the box. We put them all out on a table. Heather closed her eyes, picked a candle, and put it in the menorah. I closed my eyes, picked a candle, and put it in the menorah. We did all eight that way. The candle that was left we used as the shamus to light the other candles.

"Mom! Dad! We're ready!"

"One half a minute," Mom called. She was frying potato pancakes. The house smelled like heaven. My father put down his newspaper and came to join us.

"The menorah looks beautiful tonight," he said.

"It sure does," said Mom as she came into the room.

Heather stood next to me and looked very solemn as I sang the Chanukah blessing. I lit four candles and let her light the other four.

Then we sat down to eat. I sprinkled sugar on one of my potato pancakes and spread applesauce on another. I let Heather taste each one. She decided to eat her pancakes with applesauce. That's my favorite way, too.

After dinner I taught Heather how to

play the dreidel game. At first, she had trouble spinning the small top. But once she got the hang of it, she beat me!

Dad gave us each a package. There was a coloring book and a small box of crayons for each of us. We colored until it was time for Heather to go home.

On Christmas day, Heather invited me to her house. I brought my Sandy Goldstein styrofoam ball. Heather taught me how to bend a paper clip to make an ornament holder. She let me put my ornament up on the tree. The sequins sparkled like diamonds.

"Bee-yoo-tee-ful," Heather said. Then she giggled. You could tell she'd met Grandpa.

We had turkey for dinner with chestnut dressing. I had never tasted chestnuts before. They weren't bad. My favorite food, though, was the mashed sweet potatoes with marshmallows melted all over the top.

We had eggnog to drink, and I liked it even better than coffee-milk.

After dinner, Heather's father read the story of Christmas. Mrs. Patterson played her ukulele and we all sang around the tree. I sang all of the words to all of the carols.

Then Heather gave me a huge box that had been sitting under the tree. I sat down on the floor and tore off the paper. I took off the lid. There was another box inside. And another box inside that one.

"Heather," I groaned.

"Keep going," she laughed, "you're getting close."

Inside the last teeny-tiny box was a snowman-shaped eraser for my new blue velvet pencil.

"It's perfect," I said.

"I thought you'd like it," said Heather. "It's kind of shaped like you."

"Very funny."

We went to her room and opened the new board game her parents had given her. We played until it was time for me to go.

On my way home, I decided it wasn't so tough to be Jewish at Christmas *if* you had friends who shared with you. And maybe Sandy Goldstein didn't . . . which was why she needed a Chanukah bush.

Just then the sky opened. Thousands and millions and trillions of fat white snowflakes floated down. I turned my face up and caught some on my tongue.

"Thanks," I said softly.

I slid home on the slick walk. My shoes skated a swirly design in the fresh fallen snow.